Makeup Mess

by Robert Munsch

Illustrated by

Michael Martchenko

Cartwheel
·B·O·O·K·S·®

SCHOLASTIC INC.

New York Toronto London Auckland Sydney
Mexico City New Delhi Hong Kong Buenos Aires

The illustrations in this book were painted in watercolor on Arches paper.
This book was designed in QuarkXPress,
with type set in 22 point Plantin.

ISBN 0-439-38852-X

Library of Congress Cataloging-in-Publication Data available

10 9 8   10 11 12 13 14/0

Printed in the U.S.A.   40
This edition first printing, April 2002

To Julie Munsch,
Guelph, Ontario
— R.M.

Julie had saved up lots of money. She had saved up her birthday money, her Christmas money, and her paper route money, and she had robbed her little brother's piggy bank. All together, she had one hundred dollars.

Julie walked out the door holding all that money and her mother said, "Julie, where are you going?"

"I," said Julie, "am going to go buy myself some MMMMMAKEUP!"

Julie's mother yelled, "Oh, no!"

Julie didn't pay any attention. She ran to the drugstore, put the money down, and said, "I want some red lipstick, blue lipstick, black lipstick, pink lipstick, yellow lipstick, purple lipstick . . . I want one of everything you've got."

The man gave Julie an enormous box of makeup. She picked it up, carried it home, and took it into the bathroom. Then she said, "Now I am going to make myself BEEEEEEAUTIFUL!"

So Julie took some purple stuff and stuck it on her eyes. She took some green stuff and put it on her cheeks. She took some black stuff and put it on her lips, and she colored her hair purple. Then she put nineteen earrings in one ear and seventeen earrings in the other ear.

Julie looked in the mirror and said, "Wow, I am as pretty as a movie star!"

Julie ran downstairs and went into the kitchen. Her mother looked at her and yelled,

"AAAAAHHHHHH!"

Julie said, "What's the matter with my mother? She's acting very strange today."

Then Julie walked into the living room. Her father looked up and yelled,

"AAAAAHHHHHH!"

Julie said, "What's the matter with my father? He's acting very strange today."

Julie ran back upstairs, washed off all the makeup, and started over. This time she took some yellow stuff and stuck it on her eyes. She took some purple stuff and put it on her cheeks. She took some green stuff and put it on her lips, and she colored her hair red.

Then she put nineteen earrings in one ear, seventeen earrings in the other ear, and two rings in her nose.

Julie looked in the mirror and said, "Wow, I'm as pretty as TWO movie stars!"

She walked downstairs and went into the living room. Her mother saw her and didn't say anything. She just fell right over.

Then Julie walked into the kitchen. Her father saw her and didn't say anything. He just fell right over.

Then someone knocked at the door: *BLAM, BLAM, BLAM, BLAM, BLAM.*

Julie opened the door. It was the mailman. He didn't say anything either. He just fell right over.

"Oh, dear," said Julie. "I must have made a terrible mistake with my makeup."

Julie ran upstairs and washed everything off. Then she looked in the mirror and said, "Oh, no! I spent one hundred dollars and all I have left is my regular face. This is terrible. Nobody will think that I'm pretty!"

Julie walked downstairs. Her mother got up off the floor, and her father got up off the floor, and the mailman got up off the floor, and they all said, "Now you're really learning how to use makeup! Now you're REALLY BEAUTIFUL!"

Julie said, "But, but, but . . . I don't have on any makeup at all!" Then she ran back up the stairs, looked in the mirror, and yelled, "LOOK AT ME! I'M BEAUTIFUL WITH NO MAKEUP!"

Then Julie leaned out the window and yelled, "WHO WANTS TO BUY SOME MAKEUP?"

All the girls in the neighborhood came running and asked, "How much?"

"Three hundred dollars," said Julie.

So all the girls ran and got their birthday money and their New Year's money and their tooth fairy money, and they gave Julie the three hundred dollars.

Then they ran into Julie's bathroom and yelled, "Now I am going to make myself BEEEEEAUTIFUL!"

And Julie used some of the money to pay back her little brother, and she took the rest to the thrift store to buy lots of old clothes for . . .

DRESS UP!